Yes or No, Who Will Go?

WRITTEN BY ILLUSTRATED BY

Melody Carlson **Steve Björkman**

CROSSWAY BOOKS . WHEATON, ILLINOIS

A DIVISION OF GOOD NEWS PUBLISHERS

Yes Or No, Who Will Go?

Text copyright © 2002 by Melody Carlson

Illustration copyright © 2002 by Steve Björkman

Design by Cindy Kiple

Published by Crossway Books
a division of Good News Publishers
1300 Crescent Street
Wheaton, Illinois 60187

First printing, 2002

Printed in Canada

LIBRARY OF CONGRESS CATALOGING-IN-PUBLICATION DATA

Carlson, Melody.
    Yes or no, who will go? / written by Melody Carlson : illustrated by Steve Björkman.
      p.   cm.
    Summary: A contemporary retelling, in rhyming text, of the parable of the two brothers who say they will do one thing but do the opposite when their father needs their help in his vineyard.
    ISBN 1-58134-367-1 (alk. paper)
    [1. Parables. 2. Stories in rhyme.]   I. Björkman, Steve, ill. II. Title.
PZ8 .3 .C19475 Ye 2002
[E] --dc21
                                        2001007700
                                          CIP

11   10   09   08   07   06   05   04   03   02

15   14   13   12   11   10   9   8   7   6   5   4   3   2   1

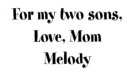

For my two sons,
Love, Mom
Melody

Mine too!
Love, Dad
Steve

A long time ago.
In a land far away,
Two babies were born.
Their names: Lee and Ray.

Lee was quite blond
With skin smooth and fair.
But Ray—he was ruddy
And had thick black hair.

The twins got bigger,
And scampered about.
But they were too little
To really help out.

Dad took them along
To the vineyard each day.
He'd tend his grapes
While they'd run and play.

The boys became older
And sometimes helped out
But when they got goofy,
It made their dad shout!

Then one summer day,
Their dad took a fall.
He hurt himself badly,
And they heard him call.

"The time is now come,
I need you," said Dad.
"To help in my vineyard,
Or things will get bad!"

"The grapes must be watered,
On each single day.
Can I count on you?"
He asked Lee and Ray.

"I've too much to do,
I cannot," said Ray.
"I've got tuba lessons,
And polo today."

"To tell you the truth,
My answer is no.
I've things to do
And places to go."

Now Lee stepped up,
Stood straight and proud.
"Have no fear, Dad."
(Lee spoke rather loud.)

"Rest and don't worry,
I'll help you," said Lee.
"Your grapes'll be fine,
You *can* count on me!"

Lee headed right out,
But got stopped by a stick
Shaped like a sword.
Lee did a quick trick.

He pretended to be
A brave, shining knight
And fought with great valor—
A flashy sword fight!

Then Lee remembered
Dad's vineyard in need
And laid down his sword
And went to proceed.

But there on the road,
A lizard was playing.
Just like a dragon
That needed a slaying!

And so once again
Young Lee was a knight.
He marched to the cave
To face the grim sight.

A fierce, fiery dragon!
A maid in distress!
Lee had to rescue
the screaming princess!

And that's how it went
The rest of the day.
Lee kept pretending
And pausing to play.

He fought off a lion,
Escaped from a trap,
Then weary and tired,
He stretched out to nap.

The vineyard was left
With no one to water.
The sun-beaten grapevines
Grew hotter and hotter.

The leaves became wilted
And droopy and dry.
Would grapes turn to raisins
And shrivel and die?

Then riding his pony,
Up trotted young Ray.
He saw the poor grapes
At the end of the day.

He leaped from his saddle
And knelt down and looked.
Dad's poor withered grapes
Looked like they'd been cooked!

How'd this thing happen?
Ray thought about Dad,
How he loved these grapes
And how he'd be sad.

Ray went back and forth
From vineyard to well.
He lugged water buckets,
And sometimes he fell!

But Ray never stopped.
He worked through the night.
He watered the vineyard
With lanterns for light.

Buckets and buckets,
It wasn't much fun,
But Ray kept on running
Until he was done!

Poor Ray got to bed
Long after midnight.
And when he awoke
The sun was quite bright.

He slogged down the stairs
All groggy and hazy
And worried his father
Would think he was lazy.

"Get in here at once!
Come now, Lee and Ray!
Get in here and listen
To what I must say."

Dad said, "When I asked,
Lee promised he'd go.
But when I asked Ray,
He clearly said no."

"But neither son did
Just what he'd said."
Their dad looked quite puzzled,
And he scratched his head.

"But one of you boys
Did what was right.
Despite what you said,
You worked through the night."

"For though Ray said no,
He did what was smart.
He did what I wanted,
He heeded my heart."

It's best to say yes
And then follow through
In keeping your word
In all that you do.

But if you say no,
Then realize you're wrong,
It's better to change
Than keep going on.

Words might not match
The things that we do.
Words can be phony,
But actions are true!

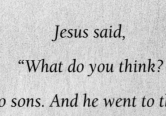

Jesus said,

"What do you think?

A man had two sons. And he went to the first an[d said]

'Son, go and work work in the vineyard today.'

And he answered, 'I will not,' but afterward

he changed his mind and went.

And he went to the other son and said the same.

And he answered, 'I go, sir,' but did not go.

Which of the two did the will of his father?"

MATTHEW 21:28-31 ESV